William Wilstinki, also known as Stinky, is new in town.

Already he's a member of the Dare Devils, and Breanna, the head of The New Bardots, wants to kiss him. Now Big M, the school principal, tells him to 'shape up or ship out'.

Life's one big dare or double-dare for Stinky, until a very cold episode with a huge iceblock gives Stinky's life a new twist.

Also by Margaret Clark

The Chickabees
Hot and Spicy
Stars
Sugar, Sugar
Far from Phoneys
Brush with Fame
Bewitched

The Mango Street Series
Weird Warren
Butterfingers
Wally the Whiz Kid
Britt the Boss
Wacky Mac
Copycat
Millie the Moaner
Bold as Brass

Other Titles
Footy Shorts
Board Shorts
Dirty Shorts
Boxer Shorts
Holey Shorts

Snap!
Crackle!
Pop!
Pugwall
Pugwall's Summer
Love on the Net

MARGARET CLARK

STINKY SHORTS

Puffin Books

Puffin Books
Penguin Books Australia Ltd
487 Maroondah Highway, PO Box 257
Ringwood, Victoria 3134, Australia
Penguin Books Ltd
Harmondsworth, Middlesex, England
Penguin Putnam Inc.
375 Hudson Street, New York, New York 10014, USA
Penguin Books Canada Limited
10 Alcorn Avenue, Toronto, Ontario, Canada, M4V 3B2
Penguin Books (N.Z.) Ltd
Cnr Rosedale and Airborne Roads, Albany, Auckland, New Zealand
Penguin Books (South Africa) (Pty) Ltd
5 Watkins Street, Denver Ext 4, 2094, South Africa
Penguin Books India (P) Ltd
11, Community Centre, Panchsheel Park, New Delhi, 110 017, India

First published by Penguin Books Australia, 2001

1 3 5 7 9 10 8 6 4 2

Text copyright © Margaret Clark, 2001

The moral right of the author has been asserted

All rights reserved. Without limiting the rights under copyright
reserved above, no part of this publication may be reproduced,
stored in or introduced into a retrieval system, or transmitted,
in any form or by any means (electronic, mechanical, photocopying,
recording or otherwise), without the prior written permission
of both the copyright owner and the above publisher of this book.

Designed by Cathy Larsen, Penguin Design Studio
Typeset in 13.5/20 Minion by Midland Typesetters, Maryborough
Made and printed in Australia by Australian Print Group

National Library of Australia
Cataloguing-in-Publication data:
Clark, M.D. (Margaret Dianne), 1943– .
Stinky shorts.
ISBN 0 14 131166 5.
1. Gangs – Juvenile fiction. I. Title.
A823.3

www.puffin.com.au

*Dedicated to all unstinky undies
and those who wear them.*

1

'Go on, Stinky,' says Mike. 'It's a dare.'

I can't believe what I'm hearing.

'You want me to ride in that *funeral procession*? You've gotta be *joking!*'

Mike, Dan and I are on our bikes riding home from school and there's this hearse with a caterpillar of cars with their headlights on behind it, going to the cemetery. Someone who was important must've carked it, because there's heaps of cars. And it must've been a long, drawn-out ceremony because they're just heading off from the funeral parlour.

'I said, and I'll repeat, I dare you to ride in behind the hearse and hang on,' taunts Mike. 'But I know you won't do it, Will-i-yum Wilstinki, cos you're a wimp and a wuss.'

I hate it when he calls me William like that. Kind of drawls it out – Will-i-yum. And I hate it even more when he calls me a wimp and a wuss.

'You're so smart, *you* do it,' I counter swiftly. 'Betcha you're not game. I double-dare you.'

'And we triple-dare you, don't we, Dan?'

Dan nods furiously, his short blond head bobbing up and down like a seriously busy dunny brush on a diarrhoea day. That's cos *he* doesn't want to do the dare, and if he sticks up for me, then Mike can get bossy and want him to do something even worse, like abseil down the town-hall building in the nuddy at lunch time, or go to the graveyards at midnight and stay there till daylight.

A triple-dare by two people means you have to do it. That's the rules.

No getting out of it.

Of course I could suddenly throw a spacko, or faint, or throw up, but then I'd be even more of a wimp and a wuss. Being a boy is hard sometimes. Like, if I was a girl I could start bawling or something, and they'd let me off.

Mrs Monroe, our school principal, is trying to stamp out daring and double-daring. (She hasn't heard about triple-daring yet!) She reckons it's a form of bullying. Mike says she doesn't know what she's talking about, because bullying's when you snot someone on the nose, or full-on beat them up, whereas daring's just – well, throwing down a challenge, making someone prove that they're not afraid to have a go, and that they're a bit of a hero. The worst thing for a boy is to be called a *girl*. That's the biggest insult you can get.

And doing dares is a real boy thing. That's what Mike says.

'It'll be time for your own funeral if you don't get a move on,' says Mike sarcastically. 'You'll be too old to do anything. So are you going for it or not?'

'Yeah,' adds Dan. 'Loser or legend?'

That's another thing. To be a legend is cool. We keep a list of who's done legendary things. And loser things. Three strikes and you're out. Like, there's five other guys want to be in the Dare Devils, just waiting for their chance. That's what Mike says. I don't know who they are, but I can't afford to be a loser. I'm two strikes down already for the time I wimped out of the free-fall jump off the bank into the river, and the time I wussed out of the throwing water bombs at Mrs Monroe's car with her in it.

Dan's a legend. He does anything that Mike dreams up. He's fearless. Some people would say he's thick, not fearless, but I can't say that cos he's a mate.

Mike's the one who gets the best ideas, you see. He doesn't actually *do* that many of the dares himself when I think about it, but every group has to have a leader and he's it. We didn't vote him in, he just sort of took the position.

'Are you a girl or what?' goes Mike.

Riding in a funeral procession's not that dreadful or dangerous. Like, it's going at snail's pace, so what's the problem? I decide to go for it.

I push off fast on my bike, ride up to the front of the procession, straight behind the hearse, and hang on to the railing thing at the side. I'm so close to the rear door that I'm almost nose-to-nose with the coffin piled with flowers. So far this has been a dead-easy dare!

Glancing behind me over my shoulder, I can see the horrified expressions on the face of the driver and his front-seat passenger directly behind me. I give a cheeky grin and a thumbs up until the person in the back seat leans forward and shakes her fist at me.

Then I'm suddenly not cocky at all.

Cos it's Mrs Monroe. Big M. In the flesh!

2

I'm standing beside my bike at the side of the road and Mrs Monroe's going mental.

She's stopped the car and leapt out, which means she's stopped the whole funeral procession. The hearse has kept on going around the corner with the driver unaware that the procession has stopped due to a major catastrophe (me), so it really doesn't matter how important the dead dude is because his procession's stuffed. A dead loss.

'I can't believe that you'd do something so

stupid, Wilstinki,' Big M yells into my face.

I drop my eyes from hers. When she gets really mad her chest heaves up and down like twin erupting volcanoes. I can't take my eyes off them. They've got a black dress over them covered by a buttoned-up black coat, but they're still heaving. She gives this choking gasp. 'I'm so upset I'm losing my breast.'

Huh? I stare at them and they're both wobbling beautifully. Then I blink and my brain cells go into forward.

She said *breath*!

I drag my eyes up to her face, and then I notice that her eyes are kind of red-rimmed and her face is paler than usual.

'You've ruined the dignity of my grandfather's funeral with your inconsiderate showing-off,' she rasps at me. 'I'll deal with you when I get back to school tomorrow. Now, on your bike before I change my mind and really lose my temper.'

'I'm sorry I mucked up your grandpa's procession,' I mumble.

'It's a cortege, not a procession. You make it sound like some sort of side show, Wilstinki.' She spits out the words over her shoulder as she stalks back to the car. All the other cars in the procession (oops, cortege) are tooting impatiently.

I turn around and see Mike and Dan watching from behind a convenient tree. I give them a thumbs-up sign, jump on my bike and go whizzing past Mrs Monroe's car and round the corner. The big grey hearse has stopped to let everyone catch up, so I slow down to give Mrs Monroe's grandpa a serious scout's salute of respect as I ride past.

'No bad feelings,' I shout to the coffin.

Let's face it, I don't need her grandpa's revenge; a ghostly visit from a dead rellie of Mrs Monroe, to give me grief. With a bit of luck his spirit is looking down from heaven and chuckling away at my bravery and daring. He probably hung onto the back of horse drays or Cobb and Co. coaches or something when he was a lad.

Come to think of it, he must've been one of the oldest living people on the planet if he was Mrs Monroe's grandpa. I thought she was about sixty herself.

My plan is to zoom round the block and leave Mike and Dan guessing for a while, so I throw a left and cut across the corner, down another side street and I'm back where I started.

'Where'd you get to?' asks Mike sourly. 'And what did the Big M say?'

'She's gunna pay me out tomorrow at school,' I say, shrugging and trying to look cool. 'How about that for bad luck? It was her grandpa's funeral. There's a dozen people dropping dead every day and having funerals and it had to be *her* rellie.'

'What a bummer.' Dan looks sympathetic.

'General purpose of a dare is to survive a major stuff-up,' says Mike. 'That's your private problem.'

He always talks in army terms, like general this and major that and private so-and-so. That's because his dad's in the army and stationed overseas.

He's busy fighting in some war or other, even though we've never heard of these wars or seen them on TV.

Once I asked Mike why he and his mum don't go and stay with his dad, like lots of other army families do, and I got a punch in the breadbasket for asking. Not a full-on, gut-crunching punch, just a friendly mind-your-own-business one.

He talks, walks and thinks army life so he must get heaps of letters and phone calls from his dad. He collects all the army-life magazines and can't wait to join up, only he's got years to go yet.

'If you were in Israel you could join the kids' army,' Dan suggested once, and got a Chinese burn for the trouble.

Mike's got a real army haircut. You know number ones and twos? Well, this is a major *one*. That's what Mike says it's called. It's so close to his head you can see the train tracks of veins connecting his brain cells to his motor neurones. His head gets cold which is why he always wears a cap. Mrs Monroe tried to make him take it off when we were singing the national anthem and his mum came up and threatened to sue her and the school council because their family's something called agnostics and not into any national pride or national religion or stuff. She was going straight to 'A Current Affair' if the Big M was going to trample on Mike's civil liberties and individual rights.

And so now Mike wears his cap all the time. And his army fatigues. And his army boots. He probably wears them to bed for all we know.

After the incident in assembly Mike dared Dan and me to wear our baseball caps backwards during the national anthem, so of course we did it for the dare.

Mrs Monroe chucked a full-on chaotic!

And of course Mum didn't bowl up to the school and complain about *my* civil liberties and individual rights, did she? Oh, no. She went berko and docked my pocket money for getting into trouble at school. And Dan's parents banned him from TV for a week for being unpatriotic.

So you can see that Dan and I have a bit of trouble trying to keep up our dare-devil image when our parents want us to be obedient little angels, but we do try.

'Dare you to ride down Devie Hill,' I say to Mike, and punch him lightly on the arm to show that it's a joke.

No one but *no one* rides a bike down Devie Hill. No one with two decent brain cells rubbing together to create coherent thought patterns, that's for sure. In fact, you'd have to be a deviant to do it.

Devie Hill is on the outskirts of our town. It's really called Deviation Hill because the road takes traffic onto a main highway in a sort of round-about way, so if the main drag is busy or jammed up, then people can take the Devie Hill route.

It's awesome. The road goes straight down. Like, *down*! Well, there's a couple of curves and also run-offs for cars and trucks that get out of control when the brakes fail, but otherwise it's dead scary. A few guys have accepted dares to ride down it and have ended up in hospital. You'd have to be an absolute maniac or a complete idiot or out of your brain to even attempt it.

'Double-dare ya,' goes Dan.

'Triple-dare ya,' I reply.

'Quadruple-dare.'

'Quintupletal-dare.'

'Sextepetal.'

'Put a sock in it', says Mike. 'Neither of you two have got the guts to do it, so why go on about it?'

'Neither have you,' I blurt.

'Your general problem, Stinky, is that you have a major reality disorder,' he says. 'Anyone who's thinking about riding a bike down Devie Hill is living in dream world.'

'Yeah,' adds Dan. 'Like, in ya dreams riding down Devie.'

'Look, I was only joking, guys,' I go. 'Can't ya tell when a guy's jazzin'?'

Mike slings one leg over his bike and shrugs. 'You talk so much bull, Stinky, it's hard to know when you're dinkum or not. There's no way you're going down Devie. And if you did, you'd be crapping your jocks for a week. Then you'd really be stinky! Stinky Stinky.'

'Yeah.' Dan follows Mike's lead and gets ready to ride.

'See ya tomorra,' I call after their departing backs.

'Not if I see ya first,' yells Dan.

Thinks he's so smart. Like, thinks he's the only kid in the universe who's ever said that.

Like I said, the trouble with Dan is he's not really bright in the brains department. And, of course, that's why Mike likes him around. General Mike and Private Dan, Mike's subordinate to boss around, just like in a regular army.

Me? Well, they've been my mates since I came to live in this town three months ago when no one else wanted to know me.

There's a saying, you can't choose your rellies but you can choose your friends.

I'm not sure that I chose these two; they sort of adopted me, initiated me into the Dare Devils. I had to drop my jocks and moon a stream of cars on the highway, then I was a devil. Just like that.

But lately I'm starting to get fed up doing dumb dares. I'm not a total idiot. I've worked out that General Mike never does anything really dangerous. He just leads his little army like a real general, and lets the mugs take the risks. Mugs being me and Dan.

I jump on my bike and head for home.

To get the heat off myself, I need a diversion.

I need more guys to join the Dare Devils, then I can move up the ranks, so to speak, to corporal or something.

Then *I* can deal out the corporal punishment!

The next day at school I get called up to Mrs Monroe's office.

It's straight after morning assembly. That's when all the exciting news about school events gets bellowed in a distorted way through the microphone. Someone should tell Big M not to swallow the microphone when she talks during assembly because the words all slur together and no one can understand what she's saying.

'William Wilstinki, come to the office NOW,' booms Mrs Monroe's voice, as the microphone crackles with fright.

I blink. That was clear enough. Me. Office. Now.

This statement signals the end of assembly and everyone prepares go into their classes. Well, except for me. It's quite odd. Mentally I'm preparing to go to the office, while physically my legs are trying to walk in the opposite direction to class with everyone else.

'Oooo, Stinky's in for it,' coos Breanna, and rolls her eyes at me, as I absolutely force my legs to walk away from the group and towards the office.

I shrug and strive to look cool. It's really important to act like you're tough and couldn't care less, even if you know you could have steel nails hammered under your fingernails, and your toenails torn out with pliers, or worse. Which of course doesn't happen nowadays, unless the principal's turned into a serial killer overnight or something. My Gran said that years ago they could beat you and strap you and cane you till you were bruised and bleeding, just for getting a spelling word wrong.

Glad the times have changed. Principals are not allowed to lay a finger on you, although they can laser-beam you with their eyeballs, which is a pretty chilling experience.

Mrs Monroe's a genius at it. She probably got an A+ for Laser Eyeballs at uni because she looks right into your eyes, bypasses the retina and goes straight for the brain.

'William Wilstinki,' she says, staring at me from behind her big desk.

'Yes, Mrs Monroe?'

I haven't had a name change since yesterday, or a face lift, so why does she have to say my name?

'You've only been in this town and at this school for three months and already you have a bad reputation.'

'I have?' I blink, surprised and pleased.

Well, it's better to be known and have a bad

reputation than be unknown and be a wimp and a wuss, isn't it? Or is it?

I consider this while she raves on about human dignity and human responsibility and the honour of the school and not behaving like a moron, while I add a few 'Yes, Mrs Monroes' into the dialogue and keep a respectful demeanour throughout the whole thing.

You see, I'm not a bad person really. I needed friends, and to get some I had to do what Mike (and Dan) told me to do, otherwise they would've dumped me like a handful of hot dog poo. Now, I'm sort of stuck with them.

'Are you listening to me, William Wilstinki?' snaps Mrs Monroe.

'Yes, Mrs Monroe.'

It's interesting how her desk's at an angle. She can see the door and she can also see into the school yard. So can I.

As she's raving on at me, her gaze drifts across to the windows and her eyes narrow as she spots a little kid playing with the bubblers on his way out to the toilet. I crane to have a look. He squirts water right up the wall and onto the asphalt in a big wet arc, then he stands back to admire his handiwork.

Mrs Monroe leaps up like she's been poked with a cattle prod and raps furiously on the window. The kid looks up, realises he's been sprung, and pelts off into the dunnies.

'Another potential ratbag,' mutters Mrs Monroe under her breath. 'This job is giving me the heebies.'

'Herpies?' I squeak. 'Isn't that – like – you get it from kissing people?'

She stares at me as if she's forgotten what I'm doing there.

'I said *heebies*. Not that it's any of your business, Wilstinki.'

Her face goes red because she's dropped her guard for a minute and revealed her innermost secret thoughts in a rash moment.

My brain's racing. Principalling's giving her heebies. They could even be related to scabies. Or rabies. So I step back from her desk just in case the heebies are highly contagious.

'If this job's giving you the heebies then you should quit being a principal, Mrs Monroe,' I offer helpfully.

'Quiet!'

She squares her shoulders and her eyes flash with annoyance as she props both hands on the shiny surface of her desk and leans forward to impale me with her laser-beam stare.

'Wilstinki, this is your last chance!' she hisses, with her twin volcanoes heaving madly. 'You shape up. Or you ship out!'

I gape at her. Shape up or ship out? Where am I supposed to ship out to? This is the only government school in the whole town.

And worse. That's navy talk.

I'm surrounded by the army. And the navy.

When does the air force arrive?

I'm back in class when the air force arrives in the form of a paper dart that slams into the nape of my neck with the force of a stealth heat-seeking missile.

'Ouch!'

Mr Cicero looks up and stares in my general direction. I don't need major grief from him right now.

Oh, NO. I'm starting to think like General Mike.

'Something wrong, Wilstinki?'

'No, sir.'

'Then get on with your work and stop gaping around the room like you're Indiana Jones trying to find the Lost Kingdom.'

The class dutifully giggles at his weak joke.

'Yes, sir.'

I try to concentrate on my maths. Zing. Another stealth missile finds its mark.

Suddenly I get the bright idea to study one of the missiles in case there's a message.

There is.

You're such a girl, Stinky.
So why don't you join our club?
Signed The New Bardots.

What is this? I turn round in my seat and glare at Breanna, the leader of The New Bardots. She blows me an air-kiss! I just shrivel in my seat. I can't believe that this is happening!

I read the second message.

Meet by the big gum tree at lunch time
and all will be revealed.
The New Bardots.

Yuck. I don't want all to be revealed. I don't want *any part* of The New Bardots to be revealed! I'm not interested in old, new or just-born Bardots being revealed! *No Bardots 4 me!*

Zing, and another winged instrument of emotional and mental destruction hits my cheek.

You're not really a girl.
You're a hunky spunky babe.
We love your image.
Breanna and The New Bardots.

Omigod, what have I done to deserve this?

'What's wrong with you, Stinky?' whispers Dan from the seat beside me. 'You're jumping around like you've got ants in your pants.'

'I haven't.'

'That'd be a good dare. To sit on a bull ant's nest,' hisses Mike from the other side. 'In fact, I dare you!'

'And I double-dare you!' grins Dan.

'Shut up,' I mutter back to them. 'There's more important stuff than dares to think about at the moment.'

I must sound really peed off because they both look surprised and then get on with their work.

I stare at the ceiling and think.

What's different about me, apart from the fact that I was hearse-surfing yesterday?

Suddenly I realise what it must be. I'm wearing my new deodorant! I've seen the ads on TV. 'N'Ice Deodorant for cool guys. Wear it, and reel in the bait. Have a N'Ice day.' There's this guy, no shirt, blue jeans undone at the waist band, leaning casually against a jetty, and all these gorgeous mermaids swimming up to him.

So what's Mum done? Been cute. Bought me this stuff! Mind you, she probably got it because it's on special.

This deodorant's extra special because you can spray it under your arms and also on your undies! It's supposed to reduce your body temperature and stop you getting sweaty and smelly. It's got this alcohol base that's been proved to keep your bum and bits and pieces cool. It's a n*ice* touch.

But surely the aroma isn't travelling from my undies through my shorts, floating across the room and up to the back row where The New Bardots hang out?

I glance around. The other girls en route to The New Bardots, ie the middle-row material, have their heads down, busily writing. Maybe it's not my new deodorant after all, or the whole room would be in a frenzy.

And it certainly didn't soften up Mrs Monroe. Although you'd probably have to spray it straight up her nostrils for it to have any effect.

So, this is even worse, because it means that Breanna, some of The New Bardots or the whole of The New Bardots, totalling five, are in love with me.

And that's a fate worse than death!

5

'I dare you to kiss Breanna,' says Mike with a big smirk.

'What?'

'She's got the hots for you, mate.'

'Yeah, well I've got the freezing colds for her and *all* girls,' I reply shortly.

'She'd be okay to kiss,' goes Dan. 'Like, she's not covered in pimples like Sarah Fellmonger.'

'I don't want to kiss *any* girls and you can centurion-dare me and I'M STILL NOT DOING IT!' I shout.

'What, Stinky, you wanna kiss BOYS?' shrieks Breanna who just happens to be cruising past while this conversation's happening near the bubblers.

I swear, the whole school stops whatever it was doing and stares in my direction, because Breanna has a voice louder than a siren at the Colonial Stadium when she gets excited.

I can feel myself going scarlet, so I stick my face into the bubbler and turn on the tap full blast. When I emerge dripping wet there's a cluster of kids waiting to see what's going to happen next.

'I dare you to kiss me,' says Breanna, with her hands on her hips.

'Yeah? Well, I dare you to go jump into a manure pit.'

'I dared you first. You can't dare me to do something else in the middle of the first dare,' she argues.

'That's right,' says Mike. 'You know the rules, Stinky.'

What a mate, NOT! I wipe my wet face with my sleeve and gaze around at the assembled crowd. Practically every kid in the school's gawping at me, even little grade-one kids with their Mickey Mouse lunch boxes.

'I double-dare you to kiss me,' says Breanna. 'And triple, quadruple and *decimal*!'

'Haven't you ever heard about boys doing the asking?' I snap at her.

'And haven't you ever heard of gender equity? Kiss me!'

'Kiss Bree, kiss Bree,' chants Mike, and starts a hand-clap to go with it.

The whole mob starts chanting and hand-clapping. If I don't do something quickly the teacher on duty will turn up to see what's going on.

Breanna's not ugly. In fact, in girl-terms she's very cute. She's got curly blonde hair, big blue eyes, long dark lashes, a small straight nose, clean white teeth. Not that I've ever really noticed the teeth before, but now that I have to kiss her, the teeth are important. I mean, if she had gunky teeth I just couldn't do it.

But then, how do you kiss a girl? Like, I've never actually ever kissed anyone on the lips except my teddy, and that was when I was four years old. What if I stuff it up? And how do you breathe when your mouth's clamped on someone else's? Like, what do you do with your nose? Do you turn it sideways and use it like a snorkel to breathe through?

And in the movies people kissing each other open their mouths like they're desperate, and they sort of nibble and gobble at each other like gigantic goldfish. As well as that, they kind of grind their chins into each other and groan a lot. What if I can't nibble and gobble and groan properly?

'KISS BREE!' The chant's getting louder,

almost reaching the volume of a Concord about to break the sound barrier, as Breanna moves right into my face and stares at me expectantly.

I shut my eyes, lean forward and aim for her cheek.

She grabs me in a headlock and plants her lips on mine. It's like being sucked by a high-powered vacuum cleaner and stuck to an octopus at the same time. I'm trying to breathe, but my nose is jammed into her cheek. I just know that I'm going to suffocate to death welded to Breanna!

I fight to break loose, bracing my hands against her shoulders and planting my feet firmly on the asphalt for leverage. It's like trying to pull up the plug in a bathful of water but finally I break the suction and fall back weakly against the wall, drawing in great lungfuls of air. Herka, herka, herrrkkkaa.

'You're a sex maniac, Stinky,' says Breanna in a voice that the whole neighbourhood can hear.

'You're an *animal*!'

Of course the reason for this great change of attitude from Breanna is the fact that Big M has just strolled around the corner to see what all the commotion's about.

'William Wilstinki, stop mauling Breanna Jones,' thunders Mrs Monroe.

'I'm not mauling her,' I argue back. 'I'm metres away. And anyway, *she* grabbed *me*!'

'He couldn't help it, Mrs Monroe,' coos Breanna in that girly-soft voice reserved to charm tree-snakes off trees and death adders into comas, 'it's his raging hormones.'

'I'll raging-hormone him,' snaps Mrs Monroe. 'Wilstinki, my office. Now!'

Raging-hormone-*me*? Omigod. Do I have to kiss Big M?

I don't.

Instead I get a lecture about male responsibilities towards females and I have to write one hundred lines of *I will respect girls at all times*.

'What about girls respecting boys?' I mutter.

'What did you say?'

'Nothing, Mrs Monroe.'

So, while everyone else does sport, I have to sit in the corner of her office and write the stupid lines. By the time I'm up to the nine- tieth one I'm ready to disrespect all girls on sight, I'm so angry and fed-up. Girls got me into this problem in the first place. Well, one girl did – Miss Bimbo of the twenty-first century, Breanna Jones.

I wriggle around for the thousandth time and try to refrain from scratching myself in a personal place. I feel hot and itchy. Probably all this sitting in one place for too long, writing stupid lines. The air can't circulate down there.

'Right,' says Mrs Monroe as the siren sounds to tell anyone who's dopey enough not to have it logged onto their subconscious alarm clocks that it's the end of the day, 'it's home time and you can go.'

I hand over my lines, listen to some more sound advice from Big M (which *is* sound, it blasts my eardrums) then I head for the corridor to pick up my rucksack.

'Dare ya to kiss Breanna again,' giggles Natalie Phyen as I sling my bag over my shoulders.

'Dare ya to kiss *yourself*,' I say.

Outside, Mike and Dan are waiting by the bikes.

'Let's burn some rubber,' goes Mike.

'Yeah, let's burn some rubber.' Echo Factor, alias Dan, nods his head.

I'm too tired from writing *I will respect girls at all times* to think of a pithy reply. And my bum feels like it's on fire, not to mention my private parts. Any minute I'm sure that they are going to explode with hot, itchy heat through the top of my head, like a volcano. I seem to be haunted by volcano images – heaving breasts and boiling bits.

I must have caught the Kissing Disease. Mono something. Surely I can't have caught a disease from Breanna Jones that quickly, can I? Wouldn't it have to incubate for twenty-four hours in my system?

Then a terrible thought hits me. Maybe I've caught heebies from Mrs Monroe! Well, I've been stuck in her company enough.

'Um,' I puff, as we reach the playground and dump our bikes on the pine-bark. 'Does anyone know the symptoms for heebies?'

'Heebies?' Dan looks puzzled.

'Describe your symptoms,' said Mike, and before I realise he's tricked me, because I didn't say that *I* had any symptoms, I'm spouting them like a fountain. I explain that I'm hot, burning, prickling and itchy, and I can almost feel something crawling across my skin.

'Yep. That's them.' He nods seriously. 'Definitely the heebies.'

'How do you know?'

'Because my brother had them once. He nearly scratched his bum off with the agony of a heebie attack.'

'What do they look like?'

'Um – a bit like fleas. You know. Small. Jumpy. Um, and they have big teeth.'

'What's the cure?'

'They hate extreme cold. You have to dunk your butt into a tub of ice,' says Mike. 'That's the only way you can get rid of them. Freeze them off. Next stop for us is Icabod's Iceworks. Let's go!'

'Yeah. I dare you to dunk your bum in ice,' says Dan.

Thick as, he doesn't have to dare me. I'm ready, willing and able.

But as we're racing along on our bikes towards the iceworks, the word *ice* seems to lodge itself behind my eyeballs. 'Have a N'Ice day!' said the slogan for the deodorant. Maybe I haven't got the heebies after all! Maybe I'm allergic and I've got a massive reaction to N'Ice.

I change my mind. Suddenly this forthcoming chill factor doesn't seem such a brilliant idea.

'Forget the ice,' I say, as we scream to a skid-stop outside Icabod's Iceworks, Pty Ltd. 'I've cooled down. Let's go down to Sandy's Shack and get a shake or something.'

'But it's a dare!' says Dan. 'You can't back out now.'

'I don't care if it's a dare.' I snap. 'I'm not having a bare bum in there!'

'You just made up a poem!' Dan gazes at me in awe.

'Girl,' says Mike contemptuously.

'What? I'm a girl for making up a poem? Wrong, mate. I'm a hero. I dare YOU to make up a poem.'

'Yeah? And I double-dare you to sit bare-bummed on ice!'

While all this arguing is going on, my butt's *on fire*, even though I'm trying to pretend it isn't. How come it wasn't like this when I first sprayed on N'Ice? It didn't start until a couple of hours later. Maybe it isn't an allergic reaction? Maybe it *is* the heebies? Maybe I should freeze them off? Doubts like little darts are pricking at my brain cells. I change my mind again.

'Okay, okay. It's no big deal. I'll sit on ice.'

We park our bikes around the corner and sneak up to the front of the iceworks. There's a refrigerated truck parked in the entrance with the doors open. Peering inside, I can see that it's half-loaded with plastic bags full of ice. The office is to one side, and through the window we can see the woman who is in charge of selling Icabod's Ice having a cuppa with the guy who's supposed to be in charge of the truck.

Beckoning us to follow, Mike crouches low and slinks around the truck and into the factory. Big swing doors lead into the freezers where the ice is stored.

'I can't see any tubs of ice,' I say, looking around and trying not to shiver, because it's as cold as the South Pole on a good day.

'There,' says Mike, pointing to a big square lump of ice that's eventually going to be crushed and bagged. 'Sit on that!'

Sighing, I walk over and sit down.

'Drop your daks or it won't work.'

'Are you sure?'

'Sure I'm sure.' Mike smiles kindly at me. 'Trust me.'

So I pull down my pants and undies and sit down. I've got to say that it's a bit of a shock to the system at first. But gradually the cold numbs my bum. The itching stops. Relief!

But something else happens. My personal bits and pieces start to shrink. I hope I don't stay like this for the rest of my life! But the relief from my sore butt is more important right now.

'Feel better?' asks Dan.

'Yeah.'

'I can see those heebies scattering in all directions,' adds Mike. 'Wow. Look at them go!'

'Where?' I twist my head around as he points behind me. I can't see a thing. Dan bends down to have a closer look. Then –

'Hey. You lot! What do you think you're doing?'

The woman comes charging through the swing doors, followed by the guy from the truck.

'I'm outta here,' says Mike and dives through the other door. Dan follows.

And that leaves me sitting like a penguin on an ice-floe with nowhere to go.

I try to get off the block of ice. But I can't. My bum seems to be glued to it. It doesn't hurt, because the cold has totally numbed my bum. When I try to stand up, the block of ice wants to come with me, and it's too heavy to lift off the ground.

'What the hell-fool thing do you think you're doing?' shouts the guy when he sees me. 'Don't you know that putting bare flesh onto ice will give you frostbite?' He's built like an Olympic weight-lifter with arms like an orang-outang.

He tries to pull me off the ice and suddenly I'm not numb any more. There's this searing pain. I bellow for him to stop, so he lets me go.

The woman is looking bewildered. This is probably the first time that anyone has actually sat their bare bum on one of her ice blocks.

Suddenly two other guys arrive from the other end of the building to see what's going on. They take one look and start laughing their heads off and pointing. I can feel my face going red with embarrassment. This is the worst thing that's ever happened to me in my entire life.

'It's not funny,' I shout.

'No, it isn't,' says the woman, suddenly looking worried because she's realised I'm in serious trouble. 'We have to get you off there, and we obviously can't pull you away from it.'

'You'll have to go into melt-down,' grins the younger guy who has a mop of curly dyed pink hair and looks like a walking Pontiac potato.

'Melt-down?'

'Well, we can't pull you off, so we'll have to melt the ice, won't we?'

'How? Light a fire?' I can't see how that's going to work.

'That's a good idea. We can use the flame-thrower!' He winks at the other.

The older man just stares at me and shakes his head. 'Perhaps we could try and hack off the ice,' he says. 'We could all lift him up, ice and all, holus bolus, and take him over to the slicer.'

I shudder. The slicer? Forget it!

'Actually, this happened to me once,' says Pink Hair.

'What, you sat on a lump of ice?' The truck driver stares at him in amazement.

'No, you nong, I stuck my tongue on the freezer door to lick off some chocolate icecream that had got spilled there, and my tongue got stuck.'

'So how did you get free?'

'Mum poured warm water on it.'

'Okay, get the hose,' says the woman. 'And make it snappy. We don't want to be sued for this kid getting frostbite. Hurry up.'

They hose away the ice around my butt with luke-warm water so that I can get unstuck. It seems to take forever. I'm shivering with the cold and my teeth are banging together like coffee beans in a grinder. The old man takes off his coat and drapes it round my shoulders.

'Now, try and stand up,' says the woman.

'I can't. I'm scared it'll hurt.'

The guy from the truck puts his hands under my armpits and gently heaves me to my feet.

I'm free.

'Doesn't look too good,' says the woman. 'His skin's all puckered and red.'

'It wwaaasss lllike thaaat beffore I saaat onnn the ice,' I chatter. 'Itt was a baad caaase of the heeeebbiiies.'

'The heebies? As in heebie-jeebies?' The old man scratches his head. 'The heebies aren't like a disease or fleas. The heebies don't exist.'

'Theeyyy donn'tt?' I stutter.

'Having the heebies is just a saying. The heebie-jeebies. It means that your nerves are on edge,' explains the woman. 'So if you say that someone is giving you the heebies, it means that they are annoying you. You know, driving you up the wall, round the twist, out of your tree.'

'Iitt doess?'

Suddenly I realise I've been tricked. Majorly.

There's a quick debate about whether they should take me straight to Accident and Emergency, or home. I explain that my grandma is an expert in homeopathy, naturopathy and herbalism and my mum has hospital experience, so home would be the best place.

I've slightly exaggerated this. Gran makes face creams out of vegies and sells them to women who don't want to get wrinkles, and

Mum used to work as a tea lady in a hospital before she got married.

I don't want to get lugged into the local hospital and have it on my record for the rest of my life that my bum got stuck to an ice block at Icabod's Iceworks. The press would hear about it and I'd be on the front page of the local paper. Everyone would know. Imagine living in this town with that hanging over your head for life.

Anyway, I convince them to take me home so that my mum can make the decision as to whether I should be taken to hospital or not.

They can see that I'm not dying of hypothermia and that I'm beginning to thaw out, so my trakky daks and undies are peeled off and put in a plastic back in my rucksack, I'm wrapped in a thick blanket and I'm driven home by Albert. I have to kneel on the front seat because I can't sit down. My bike is wedged between the bags of ice in the back. As we drive though the streets, I vow I'm gunna pay-back Mike and Dan big-time once I recover from this experience.

My butt is starting to throb now that the numbness is wearing off, and by the time the truck pulls up in our driveway, I'm feeling as if I have a massive gravel rash on my bum.

'Is there any skin left on my butt?' I ask Albert, as he helps me up the path.

'Not for me to comment,' he replies.

At least the whole street can't see my bare backside because it's hidden under the blanket I'm wearing like a tent. Albert's carrying my rucksack.

Just as we reach the front door it whips open and my gran is standing there with this astounded look on her face.

'What's going on?'

I charge past her away from the curious eyes of half the neighbourhood and head for the kitchen to heat myself up a snack of noodles.

I need warmth. In a hurry. I can hear the slow, ponderous tones of Albert telling Gran what happened.

My two-minute noodles whirl around in the microwave as I stare at them through the glass. The timer pings to tell me they are ready. I'm standing at the bench spooning them into my mouth hungrily when Gran comes bustling into the kitchen.

'What on earth possessed you to sit on a block of ice?' she asks. 'You must've known you'd get stuck to it and get frostbite into the bargain. Here, bend over.'

She lifts the blanket and peers at my butt.

'Red raw,' she says. 'That'll teach you. Well, what have you got to say?'

So I tell her how I was hot and itchy, thought I had the heebies, and sat on the ice to freeze them. She cackles away like a bantam about to lay an egg.

'The heebies? You can't catch the heebies.'

'I know that now,' I say sourly. 'Anyone can make a mistake.'

'Well, there's only one thing that's going to fix this red raw butt of yours, and that's one of my poultices.'

I groan. Gran's poultices are famous for curing things, but they are made out of the most gruesome stuff and they usually pong to high heaven.

Not only am I going to have an itchy bum, a hot bum, and a red raw bum, I'm going to have a stinky bum as well!

This is NOT a good day!

Gran makes me spread-eagle across the kitchen table while she examines my butt under the fluorescent light. Then I'm allowed to sprawl face down on the sofa and watch TV, while she makes up my poultice. I can hear her banging pots and pans in the kitchen and grinding stuff up with her mortar and pestle, which is a sort of old-fashioned way of reducing herbs and dried plants into a powder.

We came here to live with Gran three months ago because my dad ran away with another woman. It's been a bit weird, because, like I said, Gran's into all this home-grown medicine and herbs. People come to her for old-fashioned remedies which often seem to work, much to my surprise.

'The human body has become immune to most of the drugs that doctors shove into them,' she explains when I ask why her stuff is superior to modern medicine. 'My remedies are person-ally produced and not mass-manufactured, and they've been tried and true for centuries, passed on from female to female down through the ages. I'm the last of the line.'

She's the last of the line because Mum doesn't seem to have the aptitude for mixing and stir-ring and pounding and pouring. I don't think she has much faith in Gran's remedies. I heard her ask for a love potion to get Dad back and Gran said we'd be better off without him. This is probably true, seeing as this is the sixth time he's run away with a woman. A different one each time. Only this time he's been gone for the longest yet, and he phoned Mum and told her he definitely wasn't coming back. He and Lucinda were going to Queensland to grow pawpaws or something. I guess it's a bit hard to compete with pawpaws. That's when Mum cracked up and Gran said we could come and live with her.

So Mum's got a job now in Just Tarts, which is a bakery in the centre of town, and she's feeling a lot better. And looking a lot better.

Well, I don't know much about homeopathy and naturopathy and herbal remedies and love potions, but I know that Gran's skills will really be put to the test on my backside!

'And what about those mates of yours?' she asks, coming into the lounge room and standing in front of the screen so that I have to screw my head around past her to see who's winning the battle of the Qees on 'Masters of Planet Zadec'. 'Were they in on this caper? And how come they didn't stick by you when the chips were down?'

'Dunno,' I mumble. I'm not going to tell her it was a dare, and I'm not going to tell her I've got an itchy butt either. Bad enough that she's going to smear my rear end with some smelly, oozy gunk.

Gran makes a derisive sound and walks back into the kitchen to check on her brew. Before I get a chance to cover myself, Mum bursts through the door lugging bags of left-overs. She's allowed to take home the stuff that's not been sold for Gran's chooks, but we all get first dibs before the chooks get a go.

Mum sees my raw bum and goes into orbit.

'Who did this to you?' she shrieks. 'My baby!'

I hate it when she does that!

'He did it to himself,' says Gran, bustling in with her bowl of goop. 'He sat on a block of ice.'

'Why?' says Mum.

'I just felt like it!' I really don't want to go into explanations. I'm probably the only uncool male in the whole universe who's allergic to a really upmarket and trendy product like N'Ice.

Gran moves closer and I get a whiff of the goop. It stinks like moist cow manure on a hot day, rotting seaweed, and sweaty armpits. It's foul.

'You're not putting that stuff on me,' I yell. 'I'll get poisoned. My whole bum will drop off. It's disgusting!'

'Millionaires and huge corporations would kill to get their hands on this,' she retorts. 'It's my special super-healer with twelve secret ingredients.'

'Sounds like a secret recipe for the coating on take-away fried chicken,' Mum grins. 'And it smells like a chook yard. Are you sure you haven't just wandered out into the chook pen and scooped up their droppings?' Mum peers into the bowl. 'It even LOOKS like chook poo. Do you really know what you're doing?'

Gran looks offended. 'Have I ever made a bad

batch of something? Have I ever had a recipe that hasn't worked?'

'No, but –'

'Then, move aside, I'm coming through.'

Next thing she's ladling the goop onto me. I try not to throw up.

'This had better work,' I say, as Mum rushes out to get the air freshener.

I have to admit, even though it stinks, it feels cool and soothing on my raw and aching butt. Mum squirts air freshener around to get rid of the smell. It tones the room down a bit but every time I move the tiniest bit, the rotten stink rips through the air.

'The smell is dreadful,' Mum complains to Gran.

Gran sniffs. 'Smells all right to me.'

Being old, I think her sense of smell's gone. Or else she's so used to her horrible smelly potions that she doesn't notice the pong any more.

'I suppose we could try and eat our meal with pegs on our noses,' says Mum, rolling her eyes towards the ceiling.

She's got a family meat pie and three vanilla slices for us to eat.

'A maggot bag and snot blocks,' I murmur.

Maggot bag is slang for a meat pie and everyone knows that vanilla slices are called snot blocks because they look like – well, blocks of snot.

Mum pretends not to hear. Gran's made some pea and ham soup and a green salad. Instead of eating around the kitchen table, Mum and Gran perch like two birds on the edge of their chairs balancing their food on their knees, while I lie on my stomach and try to eat from that position. The soup's an impossibility, but I manage my portion of maggot bag and a snot block.

'Drink this,' says Gran, passing me a mug. 'It'll take the rest of the pain away.'

'It won't make me go to sleep, will it? Because 'Law Enforcer' is on and it's the last episode.'

She doesn't say anything, but I'm too tired to argue. I take a sip and it's nice and sweet, with spicy undertones.

The next thing I know, Gran's wrapping my bum in a thick white bandage, my head's going sort of dopey and then I start to drift off to the sounds of Mum and Gran arguing about the love potion to get Dad back.

'Hey. Look at that! A general recall on that N'Ice deodorant!'

I jerk awake.

'Whaa?' I mumble, trying to focus on the TV.

Turns out heaps of men have had an allergic reaction to N'Ice. They've developed rashes, hives, eruptions, lumps, have bought litres of Calamine lotion to cool their heat-ravaged butts, and there's talk of them suing the company that makes N'Ice. As the spokesperson for N'Ice retaliates by saying that someone has put an alien substance in that batch and sabo-taged it, I drift off to sleep with a smile on my face.

My bum might be throbbing with heat, but at least I'm a regular cool guy!

The next morning, Gran removes the bandage, tut-tuts, applies more stinky goop, and re-bandages me. I settle happily on the sofa to watch TV.

'What do you think you're doing?' asks Mum.

'Watching TV.'

'No way. You're going to school.'

'Going to school?' I squeak in disbelief. 'How am I supposed to sit down?'

'You're sitting down now,' Mum points out.

'But this is a padded sofa. At school we have

hard plastic chairs. I'll be in agony.' I look appealingly at Gran. 'And you'll need to put on more of your stuff, won't you?'

'Only if you're in pain,' says Gran. 'It's better left alone. But if you're in agony, give me a call on the school phone, and I'll come up and apply another batch.'

Omigod. I can just imagine Gran pedalling up to the school on her old two-wheeler with the basket on the front holding a big pot of goop. And where would she apply it? In the sick bay? She'd stink out the whole place and I'd be the laughing stock of the school. I'd be in absolute AGONY before I phoned her!

'What am I supposed to do about the stink?' I say sulkily, as I go to my room to get dressed for school.

'What stink?' Gran sniffs the air like a blood-hound with blocked nostrils. 'I can't smell a thing.'

'That's because your sense of smell is practically zero,' I yell. 'I can't go to school stinking like this.'

I can squirt you with N'Ice,' Mum offers, waving it at me.

'NO! That's how this whole thing started.'

'What? You mean – you got a reaction to it?' Mum's eyes light up like sensor lights, only they're sensing dollars, not movement.

'I dunno.' I retreat quickly into silence. There's no way we are joining a class action and suing N'Ice, because then my face will probably be splashed across the front of every paper in the country and on TV.

'Did you read the small writing?' says Gran, who's taken the N'Ice from Mum and peering at it through her specs. 'Not to be used by anyone under fifteen. So I'd keep quiet about you buying this stuff for our William if I was you.'

Phew. Good on ya, Gran. But that still doesn't solve the problem of my stinky butt encased in

69

its stinky shorts: the smell seems to be going right through the material.

'I can't go to school stinking like this,' I argue. 'Everyone'll think I've cacked my daks. I know my nickname's Stinky but I don't have to smell like a mobile toilet.'

'You need my Odor No,' says Gran, and scurries to get some other concoction she's made out of dried herbs and flower petals, ground to a powder with her mortar and pestle. She liberally sprinkles it down the back of my shorts. Now I smell like a cross between a gourmet delicatessen and a funeral parlour, with undertones of raw sewage. Gran spoons some of her Odor No into a plastic container and shoves it into my rucksack.

'Just in case,' she winks.

'Tell you what,' says Mum, feeling sorry for me. 'I'll drive you to school and I'll ask Harry if I can come and pick you up at home time.'

I grab my rucksack and my packed lunch off

the bench and trail out behind Mum. Getting driven in her old bomb of a car isn't exactly a status-building experience. It's a real rust-bucket and it keeps back-firing because there's something wrong with the exhaust system, but it's better than riding my bike with a half-raw bum slathered in a stinking poultice.

Mum drops me at the gate and I try to look cool as I walk up the path. Immediately I'm spotted by Mike and Dan, who both dive on me and want to know what happened.

'Thanks for sticking around,' I say sarcastically.

'Not much use us getting busted as well,' says Mike. 'Ya didn't dob, did ya?'

'No.'

'Well, then, tell us what happened.'

I exaggerate the pain and don't mention getting hosed off the ice. I sort of stretch the truth a bit by telling them how I got put into the crusher.

'Yeah?' Dan's eyes are like twin full moons.

Mike's narrow. He's not too sure if I'm telling the truth or not, and he can't really find out, can he?

'Hey, Stinky.' Breanna rushes up. 'My cousin works at Icabods and he reckons that yesterday a kid who sounds a lot like you sat with a bare bum on a block of ice and got stuck to it, and they had to hose him off.'

Big mouth!

'Wasn't me,' I go. 'Do you think I'd be dumb enough to sit with a bare bum on a block of ice?'

She shrugs, then saunters away, waggling her hips like a pregnant duck.

'Hosed off? HOSED OFF?' Mike's eyes are triumphant.

'That was AFTER the crusher.'

Dan wrinkles his nose. 'What's that smell? Sort of like a dunny.'

'Dunno.' I wriggle in my shorts and the smell wafts up past my nostrils. Oh, NO.

'The school dunnies must be blocked or over-flowing or something,' I say, moving down-wind so they can't smell me.

Mike sniffs again. 'It's YOU, Stinky. Stinky by name and Stinky by nature. Have you done a runny or something?'

'It's Gran's poultice,' I mutter, going red. 'It's a bit smelly, but it's curing my sore butt.'

'Well, you'd better sit up the back with the window open, or you'll stink out the whole class,' says Mike, as I dive my hand into my rucksack and find the extra Odor No that Gran's packed for an emergency. I tip some into the back of my shorts, and immediately the smell starts to fade.

But when I get into class I tell Mr Cicero that I feel faint and is it all right if I sit up the back in the corner with the window open. He nods. Of course this sends The New Bardots, who sit up the back, into a frenzy of giggles. A note comes winging its way to me.

I knew you cared.

I love you too.

I want to get with you.

Breanna.

Omigod, is my life ever going to be normal again?

11

It gets worse.

Just before the lunch break, Mum turns up at the school. She can't get time off to collect me because there's a big party at the town hall and she has to make heaps of sandwiches and deliver them at four. She announces this in a loud voice, standing in the doorway, holding my bike.

I wish the floor would open up and let me sink through it. Mothers can be so embarrassing.

But Mr Cicero seems to find my mother fascinating. I suppose she is if you're a desperate male. She's got this curly long brown hair that she scrapes up on her head in a top knot but strands keep escaping, so she always looks like she's sort of coming undone. And she's got the bluest eyes, a cute nose, and a reasonable figure under her loose-fitting shirt and tights. I've never really analysed it before, but I guess she's a bit of a looker.

Mr Cicero seems to think so. He just stands and stares at her like he's in a trance or something. Or maybe he's just not used to mothers crashing into his classroom gabbling their heads off and holding bikes.

'So, William, I'll see you at home after school, dear,' trills Mum, and leans my bike against the wall. 'And I hope that your – er – posterior is okay.'

Omigod!

Breanna registers 'posterior' in her tiny brain and swings around in her seat with a triumphant grin. By lunch time it will be all over the school that I sat bare-bummed on a block of ice and my Wiggly One shrank to the size of a two-minute noodle. I mean, it's normal now, but I can hardly drag it out and show everyone, can I?

Mr Cicero looks at me. 'Posterior, Wilstinki?'

'He sat on a block of ice,' says Breanna. 'With no undies.'

She can forget about love. I like a woman with loyalty, and she's got about as much loyalty as a licorice stick.

'It's just a rumour,' I say. 'There's no substance to it.'

I look to Mike and Dan for support, but they've got their heads down, busy writing. Or pretending to.

'Wilstinki, why would you sit on a block of ice?' Mr Cicero raises his eyebrows at me.

'To cool off, of course,' I blurt, before I realise that I've just admitted I did it.

'See? It WAS you!' Breanna's face is glowing with triumph.

'So? I can sit on a block of ice if I want to. What's the big deal?'

'I don't suppose,' says Mr Cicero slowly, 'that you were *dared* to do this, Wilstinki?'

'Who? Me?' I feign indignation.

'The staff at this school is sick and tired of this stupid dare stuff that's been going on lately. It's moronic. And someone will end up being badly hurt.'

He fixes Mike with a piercing stare. Mike, who's raised his head, stares back with his wide-eyed, innocent look. He's very practised at it.

Suddenly the bell rings for lunch. Mr Cicero looks at his watch. He won't want to hang about here discussing bums on ice and dares, because it's the teachers' pay day, and he'll be zooming off to do some shopping.

'Class dismissed,' he says, and we all jostle out the door.

'Wilstinki?'

'Yes, Mr Cicero?'

'I think I'd – er – better pay a home visit soon to discuss your progress.'

A home visit? Is this normal? Or is he trying to sleaze onto Mum? He probably knows she's separated from Dad: it'd be on my school record. Single-parent family. Plus a gran.

I nod. I can't tell him to butt out, get lost, not to visit because we have a flea plague or Gran's a witch or anything like that. I guess he's going to make an appointment, visit Mum, and then . . .

It's all too much. I hurry outside and of course there's the cheer squad – Breanna and The New Bardots giggling and killing themselves laughing.

'Ice Bum,' yells Breanna.

'I love you too!' I say, as I sit gingerly to eat my sandwiches.

'What's that foul smell?' She wrinkles her nose. 'Hey, it's coming from Stinky. He's cacked himself.'

'Have not!' I go bright red and shuffle uneasily, which releases more of Gran's poultice pong.

'Stinky stinks! Stinky stinks.'

Three little kids who've been lurking nearby start up the chant. 'Stinky stinks.'

'Sticks and stones may break your bones but names will never hurt you,' I say.

'You should wear a nappy,' giggles one of the girls.

'Our love is over,' says Breanna with her hands on her hips. 'I don't wanna get with someone who craps in their jocks. Yuck!'

They all walk off laughing fit to burst.

Well, one good thing's come out of all this.

I'm not getting with Breanna!

But, on the other hand, I wonder what it would have been like being the regular boyfriend of the prettiest and most popular girl in our school?

It's home time.

Gran's poultice is working, because my butt
isn't sore at all. It just *stinks* like a mobile cattle
yard. I've explained to Mike and Dan about
the poultice and they've nodded wisely
and made some sympathetic noises, but they're
still keeping their distance.

'Can you wait till I get rid of this poultice?'
I say. 'I'll ditch it in the dunnies. I don't
need it any more because I reckon I'm
cured.'

They exchange glances and Mike pulls a face at Dan.

'I won't be long,' I reassure them. 'Just give me five.'

Once in the dunnies, I peel off the poultice, wrap it in toilet paper, and dump it in the bin. I make a wad out of toilet paper, wet it and wash my butt gently. Then I dry it with more toilet paper.

'Hey,' yells Mike impatiently. 'You fallen in or what?'

'Coming!'

I adjust my shorts and hurry out. We walk our bikes to the gate (No Riding Bikes in the School Ground), and head off down the street.

'We might as well tell you the news,' says Mike over his shoulder. 'Jack's been challenged. By us.'

'You mean, Jack Trimbold?'

'He wants to do a dare,' says Mike. 'He reckons he can do anything we challenge him to do. He reckons us Dare Devils are wimps.

He says we just dare each other to do wussy stuff, like sit on blocks of ice.'

Oh, perlease. Am I never going to hear the end of this?

'So what's the dare?' I ask casually, wondering if it's walking on hot coals with bare feet, or diving into the cooling tower, or leaping across the gap between two of the town's tallest buildings.

'Devie Hill.'

'What?' I nearly run into the gutter with shock.

'Yeah,' says Dan. 'He's gotta ride his bike down Devie Hill.'

'Well, if he does it, he's crazy,' I go as I straighten the handlebars.

'He says he's gunna do it. The whole school's practically coming to watch.'

'So how come I just found out about it?' I retort snappily.

'Because we thought Mrs Monroe might wring the truth outta you if you ended up in her clutches again,' says Mike. 'And what you don't know can't hurt, if you get my drift.'

Deep inside I feel hurt. I'm one of the Dare Devils. One for all and all for one, like the Three Musketeers. So how come they didn't trust *me* with the secret when they trusted the whole school with it? Some mates! In fact, I'm starting to doubt that they *are* my mates. Let's face it, they've run away when I've been in strife, they've never stood up for me when there's trouble; in fact they've caused most of my problems with their stupid dares.

I pedal behind them, my usual place in the Dare Devil trio, as we head to the top of Devie Hill.

When we arrive there's already a crowd. Jack Trimbold's there with his new mountain bike. It's got a heap of gears. Just as well, because he'll need them to slow down, especially if his brakes give out.

'Of course one of you Dare Devils will come

along for the ride too,' he says, and spits on the footpath right near Mike's foot.

In the olden days when men challenged each other to a duel, the challenger would throw down the gauntlet, which was a thick leather glove, or would slap the other person across the cheek with it. We learned about it in history. But now, because we don't wear leather gloves, we can challenge with words. Or with spit.

'Onya, Jack,' says Breanna, who's there leaning on her bike with The New Bardots in tow.

'My bike's got dodgy brakes,' argues Mike. 'If I'd known you were going to counter-challenge, I'd have got them fixed.'

News to me that his brakes are dodgy.

'Borrow my bike,' I offer.

'My legs are too long,' he says glibly.

'My tyres are flat,' says Dan. 'I can't ride down Devie. It'll have to be you, Stinky.'

'Yeah.' Mike winks at Breanna.

I'm straddling my bike and staring at the

bottom of Devie Hill, thinking that anyone contemplating riding down it has to be a complete moron, when Mike leans over and gives my bike an almighty push. Next thing, before I can get my brain into gear and regain my balance, I'm careering down the hill.

Then Jack flashes past, going flat chat, and suddenly, grim-faced, I'm whizzing after him. There's no choice, really. I've put on the brakes and nothing's happened. My terrified brain registers that my brakes are cactus. They were okay before. Did Mike and Dan fiddle with them while I was in the dunny? No time to think, I have to survive.

I go screaming round a bend, wondering if I should steer into the next turn-out or whether my momentum will carry me straight over the edge. I roar past Jack like he's standing still and skid sideways around the corner. I must be doing a tonne. The wind factor's nearly ripping my helmet off my head.

'Stinky! Slow down!' yells Jack from way behind me. 'You're gunna kill yourself.'

'No brakes!' I bellow, as the tyres screech round the next bend.

Now I'm vertically challenged, because at this point it's a straight run, no curves, no run-offs or turn-outs. But I've made it. I'm nearly at the bottom of Devie Hill. It's probably only taken five minutes at this speed, but it feels like five hours. I've got my head down, hanging onto the handlebars and staring at the road.

Then I look up and see a truck going slowly across the road in front of me at the very bottom of the hill. There's no way I can avoid him, so I swerve the handlebars violently to the left and go ploughing straight through a wire fence and into a paddock. My front tyre hits a log, and I go flying over the handlebars. Squelch. I land head first in a fat, thick, moist, fresh cow pat.

Behind me I hear a scream, a thump and a

howl of pain. I sit up, wiping cow dung out of my eyes.

Jack's bike wheels are spinning madly in the air and he's spread-eagled on the edge of the road. I manage to stand up on my wobbly legs and stagger across to him.

'You all right, Jack?'

'Yeah.' He squints at me and starts to laugh. 'You won fair and square, Stinky, but your landing wasn't so sweet.'

He's got grazed knees and a bump on his cheek, but otherwise he's okay.

'You didn't exactly have a soft landing yourself,' I say.

'I guess now I'm a Dare Devil,' he says, dabbing at his knees with a grubby tissue.

'You can have my spot because I've quit.' I wipe off some more cow dung. 'I don't need this crap.'

He knows I'm not referring to the cow poo.

'You know,' he says, looking at me and frowning. 'I've changed my mind. I don't need to join up with those two morons. They weren't game to do the dare. You were. So, I'm with you, mate.'

There's a rousing cheer in the distance. I look up and there's all these screaming, shrieking kids charging down the hill – on foot, of course, because none of them are game to ride their bikes. It's going to take them another ten minutes to reach us, if not more.

'I don't need them,' I say, pointing up at the surging mob.

'Me neither.'

'Can you ride?'

'I reckon.'

'My place isn't far,' I say. 'Gran can put some herbal stuff on your knees and on your cheek. It's turning black-and-blue already. Her stuff stinks, but it'll fix you up in no time.'

I don't tell him that the stink coming from me is not only cow dung. Due to the fear factor, I think I really *have* crapped in my undies!

We arrive home just as a car pulls up.

'Dad!'

He piles out of a red sports car, looking neat and tidy in a smart new suit. He's got a spiky hairdo and he reeks of some fancy after-shave. Mum is just trundling up the street carrying bags of left-over buns and cakes. Her hair's falling down and her face is white with exhaustion.

'Darling,' he says, 'let me take those bags for you.'

Mum looks at him. Then she looks at me, covered in cow dung and stinking like an outdoor dunny that hasn't been emptied for a week. She looks at Jack with his grazed knees and cheek swelling up like a watermelon. She looks down at herself, with her old hand-knitted jumper and too-loose skirt, and her feet in their worn-out sneakers, then up at Dad, who looks like he's just stepped out of a fashion magazine.

'Get out of my life and don't come back,' she says to him, just as Mr Cicero pulls up behind Dad's car.

Dad gapes as Mr Cicero, summing up the situation at a glance, takes control, grabs the plastic bags, and somehow shepherds Mum, Jack and me with our bikes through the gate in a close-knit herd like a well-trained cattle dog.

Gran comes out on the porch as we straggle up the path. 'My love potion must have worked,' she mutters.

'It didn't work because Mum doesn't want him,' I whisper, jerking my thumb at Dad.

'Not *him*!'

'Huh?'

Then it sinks in and I gaze at Mr Cicero who's gazing at Mum.

'You stink, William,' says Gran. 'Get inside and take a shower while I fix up your friend.'

There's a commotion outside our gate. Dad's leaving with a roar from his engine and squeal of tyres. Breanna and The New Bardots have just arrived, puffing and panting, on their bikes, which they haven't ridden down Devie Hill but taken the short-cut across town.

'Hey, Stinky,' bellows Breanna at the top of her voice. 'You're my hero. I LOVE YOU.'

'Hussy!' says Gran loudly.

I can feel myself turn bright red as Gran ushers me in and shuts the door. I hurry to take a shower, dumping my dirty gear in the laundry basket. Should I put my yucky undies in there? I peer at them. Then I smile. I haven't cacked them. It must have just been a Stealth Bomber brought on by acute fear. Hooray. I'm not a dak-cacker after all.

When I come out of the shower I notice that Mum's bought me some new deodorant and splash cologne. It's called Jungle Juice.

Dare I?

I'll risk it. I splash lots all over myself and swipe the deodorant under my arm pits a few times.

Hopefully it'll get right up The New Bardot's noses!

And give Breanna a massive bout of hayfever, so she'll leave me alone!

About the Author

Margaret Clark is the author of many books for both younger readers and young adults, including *Pugwall* and *Pugwall's Summer*, which were made into two television series, now shown all over the world. Some of her other titles include the Chickabees series and the Mango Street books.

Until recently, Margaret worked full time as an Education Officer for the Geelong Community Health Services Alcohol and Drug Program. She is now a full-time author. Margaret has two grown-up children, a dog and a cat, and loves eating everything (except tripe), reading, writing and snoozing on the beach.

For more information see Margaret's website at http://www.margaretclark.com/

More from

MARGARET CLARK

Footy Shorts

Lennie's great-grandfather played for the Cheetahs. So did his grandfather. So did his dad. They're footy legends.

But Lennie knows he's not legend material...

More from

MARGARET CLARK

Board Shorts

Pup Morgan is a radical surfer. His dad, Mad Dog Morgan, is a surfing legend.

One day they break out, and it's six weeks of full-on surfing and the ultimate in surfaris...

More from

MARGARET CLARK

DIRTY SHORTS

The Razorblades play dirty, they fight dirty. When the Razors wreck the Top Boys' head-quarters they want to make the Razors eat dirt. But they need the help of a new Top Boy NOW.

More from

MARGARET CLARK

BOXER SHORTS

Boxer's real name is Byron Boxer, but he doesn't want anyone to know that. He has enough problems!

When he takes the train into the city with Nick, things get out of control...

More from

MARGARET CLARK

When Jack's lucky shorts wear out, his mum buys another pair – but the new shorts aren't the same. Then disaster! Mum gives his old lucky shorts away. The search is on...